MAGNIFICAT

RECENT RESEARCHES IN THE MUSIC OF THE BAROQUE ERA

Robert L. Marshall, general editor

A-R Editions, Inc., publishes six quarterly series—

Recent Researches in the Music of the Middle Ages and Early Renaissance,
Margaret Bent, general editor;

Recent Researches in the Music of the Renaissance,
James Haar and Howard Mayer Brown, general editors;

Recent Researches in the Music of the Baroque Era,
Robert L. Marshall, general editor;

Recent Researches in the Music of the Classical Era,
Eugene K. Wolf, general editor;

Recent Researches in the Music of the Nineteenth and Early Twentieth Centuries,
Jerald C. Graue, general editor;

Recent Researches in American Music,
H. Wiley Hitchcock, general editor—

which make public music that is being brought to light
in the course of current musicological research.

Each volume in the *Recent Researches* is devoted
to works by a single composer or to a single genre of composition,
chosen because of its potential interest to scholars and performers,
and prepared for publication according to the standards that govern
the making of all reliable historical editions.

Subscribers to this series, as well as patrons of subscribing institutions,
are invited to apply for information about the "Copyright-Sharing Policy"
of A-R Editions, Inc., under which the contents of this volume
may be reproduced free of charge for study or performance.

Correspondence should be addressed:

A-R EDITIONS, INC.
315 West Gorham Street
Madison, Wisconsin 53703

RECENT RESEARCHES IN THE MUSIC OF THE BAROQUE ERA • VOLUME XXXIV

Johann Kuhnau

MAGNIFICAT

Edited by Evangeline Rimbach

A-R EDITIONS, INC. • MADISON

Copyright © 1980, A-R Editions, Inc.

ISSN 0484-0828

ISBN 0-89579-131-5

Library of Congress Cataloging in Publication Data:
Kuhnau, Johann, 1660-1722.
    [Magnificat, mixed voices & orchestra, C major]
    Magnificat.

    (Recent researches in the music of the baroque era ;
v. 34)
    For solo voices (SATB), chorus (SSATB), and
orchestra; figured bass realized for keyboard
instrument; Latin words.
    Edited from a ms. copy in the hand of Gottfried
Heinrich Stölzel in the Deutsche Staatsbibliothek,
East Berlin.
    1. Choruses, Sacred (Mixed voices) with orchestra—
Scores. 2. Magnificat (Music) I. Rimbach,
Evangeline. II. Title. III. Series.
M2.R238 vol. 34 [M2020] [M2079.L6] 780'.903'2s
ISBN 0-89579-131-5   [783.4'54]   80-24236

Contents

Preface

The Composer

Johann Kuhnau (1660-1722), Bach's predecessor at the *Thomaskirche* in Leipzig, has been remembered chiefly as a keyboard composer; indeed, his *Biblische Historien* for harpsichord is one of his most well-known compositions. However, Kuhnau is also known to have written many sacred vocal compositions, and he was highly respected in his day as a composer of church cantatas. The critic Johann Adolph Scheibe (1708-1776) did not hesitate to include Kuhnau (with Telemann, Keiser, and Handel) among the four greatest German composers of his era.[1]

Johann Kuhnau was born on 6 April 1660 in Geising on the Bohemian border, not far from Dresden. Originally, his family's name was Kuhn; however, the composer seems to have adopted the new form of "Kuhnau" after his move to Leipzig, and the name always appears in this form after 1684. Kuhnau's father was a carpenter, and his mother was a tailor's daughter. Of the seven children born into this family, three became musicians. Moreover, the family seems to have been related to two prominent musicians of the day, Salomon Krügner (court musician at Dresden) and Johann Schelle (cantor at the *Thomaskirche* in Leipzig). The Leipzig chronicler Sicul identifies Krügner as a cousin of the Kuhnaus; Johann Mattheson merely refers to him as a relative and fellow countryman of the family.[2] One of Kuhnau's godparents at his baptism in Geising was Andreas Schelle, a relative of Johann Schelle.[3] Johann Schelle was also born in Geising, and as a young student he sang in the boys' choir in Dresden under Heinrich Schütz. Indeed, Johann Schelle and Kuhnau eventually worked together as cantor and organist at the *Thomaskirche* in Leipzig (see below).

As a young boy, Kuhnau was appointed as a singer at the *Kreuzkirche* in Dresden (probably in 1670), where he studied with Alexander Heringk, the organist at the *Kreuzkirche* and a former pupil of Heinrich Schütz. Another of Kuhnau's teachers in Dresden was the *Hofkapellmeister* Vincenzo Albrici, in whose home Kuhnau lived for a short time.

Toward the end of the year 1680 Kuhnau went to Zittau. Cruzianer Erhard Titius, a friend with whom Kuhnau had become acquainted at the *Kreuzschule*, had assumed the cantorate at the *Johanniskirche* in Zittau in September of that year. Kuhnau shared Titius's bachelor quarters while he completed his studies in the *Prima* class at the *Gymnasium*. When Moritz Edelmann, the organist at the *Johanniskirche* in Zittau, died in December 1680, Kuhnau temporarily filled in as organist. In May 1681, Titius died, and Kuhnau held the post of cantor until the election of a successor. Kuhnau's first known compositions date from his Zittau days. Among them is a five-voice motet, *Ach Gott, wie lästu mich erstarren*, that was the only piece of sacred vocal music to be published during the composer's lifetime.

In 1682 Kuhnau moved to Leipzig to study law at the university there. In September of that year he competed for the position of organist at the *Thomaskirche*, but he lost to Gottfried Kühnel. However, by 1684, Kühnel had died, and Kuhnau was unanimously elected organist by the city council on the third of October of that year. Kuhnau continued his law studies during his tenure as organist, and in 1688 he was qualified to practice law.

It was during Kuhnau's activity as *Thomaskirche* organist that all of his clavier (i.e., keyboard) compositions—the famous *Clavier-Übung*, the *Sieben Sonaten*, and the *Biblische Historien*—were written and published. Organ works were also composed at this time, but these were not published in Kuhnau's lifetime (although, several have been preserved in manuscript form and were published in the early part of this century).[4] During this same period, Kuhnau produced a number of literary works in Latin and German, including his famous satiric novel, *Der musikalische Quacksalber* (1700).

Upon the death of the *Thomaskirche* cantor Johann Schelle in 1701, Kuhnau was elected unanimously by the Leipzig city council to become the new cantor. He served in this post until he died in 1722. Between 1701 and 1722, Kuhnau introduced the practice of publishing texts of the main church music for Sundays and feast days. Moreover, his cantatas provided the vehicle for three other innovations in the Leipzig church music of the time: the *recitativo secco*, the da capo aria, and the tradition of the opening and closing chorale were all features of Kuhnau's cantatas.

Although references to at least eighty-five sacred vocal works by Kuhnau have been found, we know that more than half of these compositions have been lost or destroyed. The majority of the extant vocal works are church cantatas; the others are motets, two Masses, fragments of a Passion, and the *Magnificat*. Only eight of Kuhnau's vocal works have heretofore been published. Four of the church cantatas, *Gott sei mir gnädig nach deiner Güte, Ich freue mich im Herrn und meine Seele ist fröhlich, Wenn ihr fröhlich seid an euren Festen*, and *Wie schön leuchtet der Morgenstern*, have been edited by Arnold Schering and appear in *Ddt*, 1. *Folge*, *Bd*. 58/59. Both *Gott sei mir gnädig* and *Wie schön leuchtet* appear also in practical editions.[5] Another cantata, *Ich habe Lust abzuscheiden*, appeared in the *Organum* series, edited by Max Seiffert.[6] This edition is now out of print. Quite recently, two more cantatas have appeared in practical editions: these are the solo cantata *Ich hebe meine Augen auff* and the chorale cantata *Christ lag in Todesbanden*.[7] The motet *Tristis est anima mea* has received more attention than any other vocal work by Kuhnau, and it has been published frequently both in Germany and the United States.[8]

Because the majority of Kuhnau's vocal works are cantatas, and because Kuhnau's vocal style is well demonstrated in these works, the following discussion will focus on them. Stylistically, Kuhnau's vocal works make a transition from the seventeenth to the eighteenth centuries. Throughout his life, Kuhnau had feared succumbing to the operatic style, and thus he sought to maintain the ideals of his predecessors in church music. Until fairly late in his career Kuhnau avoided using recitatives and da capo arias so he could, as he wrote in an essay in his book of cantata texts for 1709-1710, "more easily combat the suspicion of theatrical music. . . . In the church style [one] seeks to stir up in the hearer holy devotion, love, joy, sadness, wonderment and similar things. . . . The theatrical style gives to the worldly-minded, however, always more and more nourishment for their carnal desires."[9] However, aspects of eighteenth-century style also emerge in Kuhnau's compositions in that he transformed the old chorale cantata and choral concertato by making use of new madrigal poetic interpolations. Such interpolations first appeared after 1700 (beginning with Erdmann Neumeister), when poets prepared cantata texts. Neumeister, in particular, shifted the emphasis from direct quotations of biblical texts to their poetic interpretation. Thus, texts consisting of free paraphrases of biblical text either totally replaced the biblical quotations or served as poetic insertions. These paraphrases of biblical texts were termed *madrigalian* as they appeared in the underlay to the church cantata and the choral concerto.

The typical Leipzig festival cantata in the latter half of the seventeenth century was scored for a five-voice choir, five soloists, and an orchestra with an instrumentation of two violins, two or three violas, bassoon, two clarini, two or three trombones, timpani, and a continuo comprised of bass viol and organ. However, Kuhnau's cantata-settings were somewhat more elaborate than what was considered "typical" at that time, and at first the congregations in Leipzig were shocked at the composer's use of longer opening instrumental sonatas, longer instrumental introductions to arias, and more elaborate vocal writing.

Indeed, in composing these works for the Thomaskirche, Kuhnau was responsible for the basic structure of the Leipzig church cantata as later used by Bach. He defined the roles of the recitative and aria and, as we shall see, freed the melody of the old *Lied* in the new da capo aria so that this melody became a more lyrical outpouring of song. The old *Lieder* (solo songs) had a popular simplicity and generally made use of a syllabic setting of the text. In Kuhnau's arias, this simple style gave way to a more elaborate vocal treatment of the melody with some use of coloratura, textual repetition, and melodic variation. Although Kuhnau criticized the recitative and da capo aria for having secularizing effects on church music, it was he who gave this form a secure position in the Leipzig church cantata.

In the cantatas, as in Kuhnau's other extant vocal works, the choruses are written in concertato style, with alternating homophonic and fugato passages. There is also the contrast of solo and tutti in these choruses, with solo voices most often used at the beginning of fugato passages. True choral fugues are rare, and homophonic writing predominates. Arias are through-composed, strophic, or da capo, and they are usually accompanied by one or two concertizing instruments; although occasionally a larger accompanying ensemble is used. Moreover, there are quite a number of arias that call for simple continuo accompaniment. Duets in the cantatas are similar in style to solo arias; however, there is also some imitative writing for the two solo voices, especially at the beginning of phrases. As may be seen from the following remarks on specific aspects of Kuhnau's *Magnificat*, this work, too, illustrates Kuhnau's typical vocal style.

The Magnificat

The *Magnificat* is the largest of Kuhnau's extant vocal works. It calls for four soloists, a five-voice choir, and a festival orchestra of three clarini, timpani, two oboes, two violins, two violas, and continuo (organ and bass viol). A manuscript presently in the Deutsche Staatsbibliothek in East Berlin is the only known source of this work. This source is a full score in the hand of Gottfried Heinrich Stölzel, who was *Hofkapellmeister* in Gotha and a composer in his own right. The manuscript bears no date, and there is no specific indication of the occasion for which the *Magnificat* was written. However, because this is the only Magnificat that Kuhnau composed, and because it is an elaborate setting, it is probable that this work was intended for use at Christmas. If the *Magnificat* was performed during the Christmas season in Leipzig, it is likely that Christmas hymns were inserted between certain movements. Such insertions of German Christmas (or Easter) hymns may have been a tradition in Leipzig, and Philipp Spitta has written that Kuhnau's Christmas music was connected closely with Leipzig church customs.[10] Indeed, inserting

Christmas or Easter hymns into Magnificats is a practice that goes back at least as far as Praetorius, whose *Megalynodia Sionia* of 1611 contains fourteen Latin Magnificats, three of which have German Christmas or Easter hymns inserted between their movements. If Kuhnau followed this practice, his logical choice of a source for the inserted hymns would have been his cantata *Vom Himmel hoch*. This work is unique among Kuhnau's church cantatas in that it is comprised simply of four choral movements on texts of four Christmas hymns—"Vom Himmel hoch," "Freut euch und jubiliert," "Gloria in excelsis," and "Virga Jesse floruit." The four choruses of Kuhnau's *Vom Himmel hoch* are all in the key of C major, the key of his *Magnificat*, and thus they could easily have been inserted between certain movements according to this practice. That this custom continued in Leipzig after Kuhnau's time is demonstrated by the fact that J.S. Bach inserted choruses setting the texts of the same four Christmas hymns (i.e., those set in Kuhnau's *Vom Himmel hoch*) into his *Magnificat*, written in 1723.

It is interesting to compare Kuhnau's setting of the Latin Magnificat with one of Johann Krieger's many Magnificats and with Bach's *Magnificat* because these works represent three "generations" of Magnificat-composition, and thus a continuum of stylistic characteristics can be traced through these three works. The earliest of these settings is the one composed by Johann Krieger in 1685.[11] Four sections of the text are set for chorus: "Magnificat," "Fecit potentiam," "Sicut locutus," and "Sicut erat." The remaining verses are set for solo voices, including a trio ("Deposuit") and a duet ("Suscepit"). Kuhnau's *Magnificat*, written some time after Krieger's, is quite similar in its distribution of choruses and arias. With one exception, an additional chorus for the verse beginning "Quia fecit," Kuhnau sets the same textual portions for chorus as Krieger did (see below). Bach's *Magnificat*, written in 1723, shows similarity to Kuhnau's setting and hence also to Krieger's in its choice of choruses and arias. Bach sets five choruses, just as Kuhnau does, but his second chorus uses the "Omnes generationes" text instead of the "Quia fecit" text. Bach sets the "Quia fecit" for bass solo. In addition, Bach sets the entire "Gloria Patri" text for chorus, whereas Kuhnau sets only the second portion ("Sicut erat") for chorus. This kind of comparison seems to indicate that Kuhnau was probably acquainted with and influenced by Krieger's *Magnificat* just as Bach was with Kuhnau's *Magnificat*. Kuhnau's *Magnificat* is probably a late work of the composer, and it contains some of his best vocal writing.

The Choruses

After a brief twelve-measure instrumental introduction, solo voices from within the chorus state the first phrase of the opening chorus, "Magnificat." Then, at m. 16, the tutti chorus repeats the opening phrase.

The remainder of the text of the first chorus is treated homophonically. A da capo of the opening instrumental section appears at the end of the chorus (m. 35). The second chorus, "Quia fecit," opens with a short fugato (beginning at m. 126). However, the fugal writing is of short duration, and by the time all the voices have entered, the fugato comes to an end. The middle chorus, "Fecit potentiam," opens with a short brass fanfare (beginning at m. 196), creating a martial atmosphere that emphasizes the meaning of the text. A fugato opens the chorus "Sicut locutus" (at m. 334) as well as the final chorus, "Sicut erat" (at m. 404). In the "Sicut erat," as in the opening "Magnificat," there is alternation of solo and tutti sections—the solo voices are indicated at the opening of the fugato in each case. Kuhnau's facility in writing double counterpoint is exhibited in this final chorus (mm. 418 ff. and mm. 434 ff.).

The Arias and Duets

The first soprano aria, "Et exsultavit" (beginning at m. 54), has a flowing siciliano rhythm. It is a motto aria with a da capo of the nine-measure instrumental introduction (mm. 45-54) occurring at the close (mm. 84-93). This plan of instrumental introduction and da capo is followed in the two tenor arias, "Et misericordia ejus" (mm. 159-195) and "Suscepit Israel" (mm. 256-333). On the other hand, the alto aria, "Quia respexit" (mm. 93-125), has no instrumental introduction, no motto beginning, and no da capo form. Here, the voice enters after one downbeat chord in the strings and proceeds, with some use of melodic sequence, in through-composed style.

The duet for soprano and bass, "Deposuit" (mm. 220-232), illustrates Kuhnau's imitative treatment of the two solo voices as well as some typical baroque-period text-painting on the word "deposuit." The duet for soprano and alto, "Esurientes" (mm. 233-255), that follows "Deposuit" without pause, uses the accompanying strings in ritornello fashion.

Kuhnau's setting of the "Gloria Patri" (mm. 368-439) is unique in that it makes use of both soloist and chorus. Whereas in most baroque settings the full chorus sings the entire "Gloria Patri, gloria Filio, gloria Spiritui" text, here the composer writes a setting of these words for bass solo; the chorus does not enter until the words "Sicut erat." Kuhnau may have been influenced by Johann Krieger's *Magnificat* of 1685, which has this same arrangement (see above).

The Edition

Few editorial additions or emendations were necessary for the preparation of the *Magnificat*. No dynamic marks were added by the editor, except where Stölzel obviously omitted a mark in some of the individual lines. Bracketed figured-bass numerals and bracketed accidentals are editorial. In the manuscript a sharp sign was generally used to cancel previously indicated flats. In this edition, all such sharp signs have been changed to naturals. In the source, fermatas are indicated only at the top of the first stave of the full score and occasionally below the bottom stave. In this edition, these signs are indicated in all the parts. The viola II part was originally written in the tenor clef; this has been editorially changed to alto clef in order to correspond with the viola I part. Beaming and stemming have been tacitly regularized in the edition.

Orthography follows the *Magnificat* text as given in the *Liber Usualis*. Text underlay in homophonic sections of the choruses appears in the manuscript only in either the soprano or the bass voice: measures 13-32 in the opening chorus have text only in the soprano; text is given in the bass only in mm. 141-150, mm. 198-207, mm. 211-219, mm. 424-430, and mm. 435-439.

The realization of the continuo line appears in cue-sized notes. The lowest pitch in the bass clef is that indicated by Kuhnau as the continuo part. The editor has tried to make the style of realization playable and faithful to the original figures.

Critical Notes

The following entries document discrepancies between the present edition and the source (Deutsche Staatsbibliothek, East Berlin). The following abbreviations are used below: vn. = violin, vla. = viola, ct. = continuo, T. = tenor, B. = bass. Pitches are indicated according to the usual system wherein c' = middle c, c" = the c above middle c, and so forth.

M. 9, vla. II, final note is e'. M. 11, vla. II, final note is e'. M. 40, vla. II, final note is e'. M. 42, vla. II, final note is e'. M. 93, vla. II, note 2 is e'. M. 165, ct., final note, figured bass is $^6_\#$. M. 187, T., note 2 is g. M. 281, vn. I, final note is d". M. 291, ct., final note, figured bass is $^6_5$. M. 293, ct., final note, figured bass is $^6_\#$. M. 318, T., notes 2 and 3 are b and a. M. 394, B., note 10 is f-natural. M. 395, vn. II, note 4 is f"-natural.

Acknowledgments

Preparation of this manuscript was made possible by a post-doctoral fellowship given by the American Association of University Women and with the cooperation of the Deutsche Staatsbibliothek.

Evangeline Rimbach
Concordia College
River Forest, Illinois

June 1980

Notes

1. See Fr. Wilhelm Riedel, "Johann Kuhnau," in *Musik in Geschichte und Gegenwart* (Kassel, 1949-1969), VII: col. 1884.
2. Richard Münnich, "Kuhnau's Leben," in *Sammelbände der Internationalen Musikgesellschaft* (1901/1902), p. 478.
3. Ibid., p. 474.
4. See Karl Straube, *Choralvorspiele alter Meister* (New York, 1951), pp. 94-97; and Max Seiffert, ed., *Organum* (Leipzig: Kistner & Siegel, n.d.), IV: no. 19.
5. See J. Kuhnau, *Gott sei mir gnädig* (Hilversum: Harmonia-Uitgave, no date or editor given); and J. Kuhnau, *How Brightly Shines the Morning Star*, ed. Horace Fishback III (New York: H.W. Gray Co., Inc., 1961).
6. J. Kuhnau, *Ich habe Lust abzuscheiden*, in *Organum*, ed. Max Seiffert (Leipzig: Kistner & Siegel, 1928), I: no. 14.
7. See J. Kuhnau, *Ich hebe meine Augen auff*, ed. Harald Kümmerling (Cologne, 1964); and J. Kuhnau, *Christ lag in Todesbanden*, ed. Horace Fishback III (Glen Rock: J. Fischer & Bro., 1966).
8. See, for example, J. Kuhnau, *Sorrow Doth Vex Now My Spirit*, ed. Walter E. Buszin (St. Louis: Concordia Publishing House, 1951).
9. Bernhard Friedrich Richter, "Eine Abhandlung Joh. Kuhnaus," *Monatshefte für Musik-Geschichte* 34 (1902): 147-150, quotes this statement from Kuhnau's essay.
10. Philipp Spitta, *Johann Sebastian Bach* (London, 1899), II: 372.
11. *Ddt*, 1. *Folge*, Bd. 53/54, pp. 1-23.

Plate I.   Johann Kuhnau, *Magnificat*. First page of score.
(Courtesy, Deutsche Staatsbibliothek, East Berlin)

MAGNIFICAT

Magnificat

7

5 7 5   5
  5 4 3   4 3

6

5 7 5   5
  5 4 3   4 3

-ta- tem an- cil- lae, an- cil- lae, an- cil- lae, an- cil- lae_ su- ae:

ec- ce_ e- nim ex hoc, ex_ hoc,   ec- ce_ e- nim ex hoc, ex_

o-mnes ge-ne- ra- ti- o- nes, o- mnes

ge-ne-ra-ti- o- nes.   ec-ce__ e-nim ex hoc, ex_hoc,   ec- ce__

e- nim ex hoc, ex__hoc be- a-   tam, be- a-   tam me di-cent__

o- mnes, o-mnes ge-ne-ra- ti- o-   nes.

135

est,   qui po- tens est,   qui po- tens est, qui

est,   qui po- tens est,   qui po- tens est, qui

est,   qui po- tens est,   qui po- tens est, qui

est,   qui po- tens est,   qui po- tens est, qui

est,   qui po- tens est,   qui po-

po- tens est, qui po- - tens est, qui po- tens est, qui po- tens est, qui

po- tens est, qui po- - tens est, qui po- tens est, qui po- tens est, qui

po- tens est, qui po- - tens est, qui po- tens est, qui po- tens est, qui

po- tens est, qui po- - tens est, qui po- tens est, qui po- tens est, qui

- tens est, qui po- - tens est, qui po- tens est, qui po- tens est, qui

6   [6]   6   [6]

27

28

30

Et___mi- se- ri- cor- - di- a e- jus,

et___ mi- se- ri- cor- di- a e- jus a pro-ge-ni- e in pro-ge-ni-es,

a pro- ge- ni- e in pro-ge-ni- es ti- men-

Fe- cit po-ten-ti-am in bra- chi-o

Fe- cit po-ten-ti-am in bra- chi-o

Fe- cit po-ten-ti-am in bra- chi- o

Fe- cit po-ten-ti-am in bra- chi- o

Fe- cit po-ten-ti-am in bra- chi- o

44

su- um,___ su- sce- pit___ Is- ra-el, su- sce- pit___ Is- ra-el

pu- e-rum, pu- e-rum___ su- um,

-cor- - di- ae___ su- ae, mi- se- ri-

-cor- di-ae su - ae,

su- ae.

54

340

pa- tres no- - stros, ad pa- tres__ no- stros, ad pa- tres__

Si- cut lo-cu-tus est ad pa- tres, ad pa- tres__ no- stros, ad pa- tres__

pa- tres__ no- stros, si- cut lo-cu-tus est ad pa- tres no- stros, ad pa- tres no- stros, ad

pa- tres, ad pa- tres__ no-stros, si- cut lo- cu-tus est ad pa- tres, ad pa- tres no- stros, ad

pa- tres__ no- stros, si- cut lo-cu-tus est ad pa- tres__ no- stros, ad pa- tres__ no- stros, ad

6   5   6   5   5   6
     3

55

56

58

60

- ri- a, glo- ri- a,

7 6   7 6   7 6   7 6   5 4   7 6
       5   #

380

glo- ri- a, glo-ri-a

7 6   7 6   7 6   5 7 6   6 7 7   6   6 7 4   7 6
              5   #   5   #   5   #

Pa- tri,___ glo- ri- a, glo- ri- a Fi- li- o, glo- ri- a et Spi- ri- tu- i San-

-cto! Glo- ri- a, glo- ri- a Pa- tri, glo- ri- a Fi- li- o et Spi- ri- tu- i San-

-cto!
Glo- ri- a Pa- tri, glo- ri- a Fi- li- o, glo-ri-a Spi-ri- tu-i, glo-ri- a Spi-

-ri- tu-i San- cto!
Glo- ri- a, glo-

ri- a, glo- - ri- a.

70

-ci- pi- o, et nunc, et nunc, et | sem- per, et in sae- cu-la sae-cu- | lo- rum. A— men,

a- men, a— men, a-men, | a- men, a— men, a- men, | a- men, a- men, a- men,

-ci- pi- o, et nunc, et nunc, et | sem- per, et in sae- cu-la sae-cu- | lo- rum. A— men,

-ci- pi- o, et nunc, et nunc, et | sem- per, et in sae- cu-la sae-cu- | lo- rum. A— men,

- men, a- | - men, a- | - men, a— men,

76